Bearded Dragons

Marco Andres

PowerKiDS press

New York

Published in 2018 by The Rosen Publishing Group, Inc.
29 East 21st Street, New York, NY 10010

First Edition

Editor: Melissa Raé Shofner
Book Design: Rachel Rising

Photo Credits: Cover Eric Isselee/Shutterstock.com; Cover, p. 1 Spyder 1960/Shutterstock.com;
p. 5 Siarhei Kasilau/Shutterstock.com; p. 7 Kike Fernandez/Shutterstock.com; p. 9 ukjent/Shutterstock.com;
p. 11 Michelle D. Milliman/Shutterstock.com; p. 13 Licvin/Shutterstock.com; p. 14 chinabzyg/Shutterstock.com;
p. 15 kungverylucky/Shutterstock.com; p. 17 F STOP IMAGES/Shutterstock.com; p. 18 Kuttelvaserova Stuchelova/Shutterstock.com;
p. 19 Maica/Getty Images; p. 21 Stephen Simpson/Getty Images; p. 22 likekightcm/Shutterstock.com.

Cataloging-in-Publication Data
Names: Andres, Marco.
Title: Bearded dragons / Marco Andres.
Description: New York : PowerKids Press, 2018. | Series: Our weird pets | Includes index.
Identifiers: ISBN 9781508154242 (pbk.) | ISBN 9781508154181 (library bound) | ISBN 9781508154068 (6 pack)
Subjects: LCSH: Bearded dragons (Reptiles) as pets–Juvenile literature.
Classification: LCC SF459.L5 A53 2018 | DDC 639.3'955–dc23

Manufactured in the United States of America

CPSIA Compliance Information: Batch #BS17PK: For Further Information contact Rosen Publishing, New York, New York at 1-800-237-9932

Contents

Pet Dragons

If you tell your friends you have a pet dragon, they probably won't believe you. However, if you own a bearded dragon, it would be true! They aren't real dragons, but they do make excellent pets—even for kids!

Bearded dragons are a type of lizard from Australia. They were brought to the United States in the 1990s. They quickly became popular pets because they're calm and easy to care for. Is a bearded dragon the right pet for you?

PET FOOD FOR THOUGHT

Bearded dragons sleep at night and are active during the day.

Don't be afraid of their **spikes**. Bearded dragons usually don't mind being held.

Lizards with Beards

Bearded dragons have spiky scales covering their neck. If a bearded dragon senses danger, it will stand still and puff out its throat. This makes the lizard look like it has a big beard, which is where its name comes from.

Bearded dragons have short legs, but they can run up to 9 miles (14.5 km) per hour. Their tail is usually about half the length of their body. Their body has spikes down both sides.

PET FOOD FOR THOUGHT

Both male and female bearded dragons have spiky beards.

Bearded dragons puff out their throat to look scary, but they're actually very gentle animals.

7

Colorful Creatures

Bearded dragons come in many colors. They may be tan, brown, gray, red, white, orange, or yellow.

Bearded dragons can change the color of the skin on some body parts! This helps them stay warm or keep cool. For example, to cool off in the hot desert sun, a bearded dragon may make the skin on its back a lighter color. Their colors may also help them hide from predators and attract **mates**.

PET FOOD FOR THOUGHT

Some people **breed** bearded dragons to have smaller scales. These dragons will feel and appear smoother and their colors may be brighter.

People may breed bearded dragons for beautiful, bright color patterns. Dragons of certain colors may cost more than others.

Buying a Bearded Dragon

There are nine species, or kinds, of bearded dragons in the wild. In the United States, most of the bearded dragons sold as pets are a species called central bearded dragons.

Bearded dragons can be purchased at many pet stores. You may also be able to adopt one from a local **animal shelter**. If you buy a bearded dragon from a breeder, make sure the business is **reputable** and the breeder takes good care of their animals. Don't be afraid to ask questions about your new pet.

PET FOOD FOR THOUGHT

Bearded dragons can live up to 10 years. With excellent care, some live even longer. Keep this in mind when deciding if you want one for a pet.

You can guess the age of a bearded dragon by measuring how long it is. This one is just a baby. Longer dragons are generally older, and shorter dragons are generally younger.

Bearded dragons can grow up to 24 inches (61 cm) long, so they need a big **tank** to live in. Set up the tank before you bring your new pet home. Start by adding a few inches of sand. For younger dragons, a special carpet may be safer.

Your bearded dragon needs a heat lamp to keep it warm. It also needs a place to hide and cool off, such as under a piece of wood or a rock. Add branches to the tank so your dragon can climb or hide.

PET FOOD FOR THOUGHT

You should clean any waste from the tank at least once a week and completely change the bedding once a month.

Bearded dragons prefer to live alone. They like to protect their territory and may fight other lizards in their tank.

13

Time to Eat!

Bearded dragons are omnivores. This means they eat both meat and plants. Crickets are one of their favorite foods. You can buy crickets at the pet store to feed to your bearded dragon each day. Younger dragons need to eat more crickets than older ones because they're still growing.

Part of your dragon's diet should be fresh fruits and vegetables. You shouldn't feed it avocados, oranges, or iceberg lettuce, though. These foods aren't good for bearded dragons.

PET FOOD FOR THOUGHT

A general rule is that any fruit or vegetables should be chopped into pieces smaller than the space between your bearded dragon's eyes. This is so your pet doesn't choke. Bugs should also be this size or smaller.

Bearded dragons need a good mix of fresh vegetables, fruit, and meat. You can feed your pet crickets, cockroaches, and different types of worms.

Health and Wellness

There are a few interesting **behaviors** to watch for in your pet bearded dragon. In the fall or winter, your dragon may sleep more and eat less. This is called brumation. It's normal, but not all dragons do it.

Bearded dragons also **shed** their skin a few times a year. Younger dragons grow faster, so they shed more. When shedding occurs, your dragon's eyes might look puffy and their color will be dull. Don't pick at your dragon's flaky skin.

PET FOOD FOR THOUGHT

It's important that your bearded dragon stays warm enough. Heating lamps should be kept outside the tank so your dragon doesn't get burned.

It's a good idea to give your bearded dragon a quick, warm bath once every four to eight days. This will keep it clean and **hydrated**. Don't use soap though—water is all you need.

Handle with Care

Bearded dragons are gentle animals that often enjoy being held. Pick up your dragon carefully by sliding your hand under its belly. Never hold your pet too tightly or grab it by the legs or tail.

You may have heard warnings about something called salmonella. Salmonella is bacteria that can be found in the waste of many lizards. It's not likely that your dragon will make you sick. Still, you should always wash your hands after handling your pet, just to be safe.

PET FOOD FOR THOUGHT

Many lizards can regrow their tail if it breaks off. Bearded dragons don't have this ability.

Bearded dragons rarely bite, but they might accidently scratch you with their sharp claws.

19

Fun with Your Dragon

Bearded dragons can be really fun! Unlike many other small pets, they don't need to stay in their tank all the time. Bearded dragons like to go outside for walks. They may also enjoy car rides. Just make sure your pet isn't running around loose or the driver might crash.

Some bearded dragons enjoy playing with toys such as small balls. Bearded dragons also love to swim! You can run a small amount of warm water into your bathtub and watch your pet splash around.

PET FOOD FOR THOUGHT

You can buy a special **harness** to take your bearded dragon outside for walks.

Give your bearded dragon lots of attention. Your pet will soon begin to recognize you!

21

Bearded Dragon Care Fact Sheet

- Bearded dragons need a large tank to live in.

- Don't keep more than one dragon in a tank.

- Mist the tank lightly with water once a day to help keep your dragon hydrated.

- Make sure your pet always has water to drink.

- Clean your dragon's tank at least once a week.

- Bearded dragons love to eat fruits, vegetables, and bugs such as crickets.

- Make sure food is small so your pet doesn't choke.

- Always be gentle when handling your bearded dragon.

Glossary

animal shelter: A place where people take lost animals or animals without an owner.

behavior: The way a person or animal acts.

breed: To bring a male and female animal together so they will have babies.

harness: A set of straps that goes around an animal's body; often used to control it.

hydrated: Having a healthy amount of water in the body.

mate: A partner for making babies.

reputable: Being well thought of, respected, and in good standing.

shed: To get rid of skin, fur, or feathers.

spikes: Sharp, pointy things shaped like a spear or a needle.

tank: A large container, often made of glass, that holds water or other material.

Index

Websites

Due to the changing nature of Internet links, PowerKids Press has developed an online list of websites related to the subject of this book. This site is updated regularly. Please use this link to access the list: www.powerkidslinks.com/owp/drag